W9-CER-025

Veronica Meets Her Match

Veronica Meets Her Match

Nancy K. Robinson

SCHOLASTIC
HARDCOVER

Scholastic Inc.
New York

Library of Congress Cataloging-in-Publication Data

Robinson, Nancy K.
Veronica meets her match

Summary: Veronica's fervent attempts to gain peer acceptance continue
as she claims the new girl as her own special friend. Sequel to *Just Plain
Cat, Veronica the Show-off*, and *Veronica Knows Best.*
[1. Friendship—Fiction.]   I. Title.
PZ7.R56754Vdm   1990   [Fic]   89-49543
ISBN 0-590-41512-3

12 11 10 9 8 7 6 5 4 3 2 1   0 1 2 3 4 5/9

Printed in the U.S.A.   37

First Scholastic printing, September 1990

To Eva — dead center, front row . . .

List of Chapters

Chapter 1

The Empty Seat

Veronica was shocked.

"But what about *me*?" she asked.

Her best friend, Hilary, blinked.

"You simply cannot take any more lessons if you want to continue this friendship." Veronica's voice was trembling with rage.

"But I want to take pottery," Hilary said.

"Yes, and I suppose you want to keep on taking piano, ballet, and karate lessons twice a week. You can't do everything, you know."

"Well, ballet helps with karate, and piano helps with ballet . . . ," Hilary said.

"Now you are going to have lessons every single day." Veronica felt sick.

Veronica was desperate for someone to play with after school. Her afternoons were lonely. Mrs. Moore, her old baby-sitter, had been fired for watching too many soap operas — "a bad influence on Veronica" — and for taking Veronica to the racetrack one Saturday afternoon.

Veronica had never cared very much for Mrs. Moore, but now she found herself missing her. Her mother had gone on a ski trip and had hired a young law student named Barbara to housesit and keep an eye on Veronica. Barbara had a French manicure twice a week and talked on the telephone all the time.

"Here comes the little creature now," Veronica had heard her say several times when she arrived home from school.

Veronica stared out the window of the bus and thought how inconsiderate it was of Hilary to break the news to her right this minute.

It was a cold Monday morning at the end of January. Veronica had been planning to study on the bus. She had a mathematics test first period and she wanted to impress her new fifth-grade teacher.

Veronica was used to being the class pet — a position that seemed to go along with being the smartest. Miss Penny had started teaching her class this term. She had not yet noticed that Veronica was her star pupil.

"And what exactly do you expect to accomplish by taking pottery?" Veronica asked Hilary. "What do you expect to have to show for it?"

"Pots, Veronica," Hilary said softly. "I am going to have pots to show for it."

Veronica decided to shift her argument. "There are a million pots in this world. What makes you think *you* will be any good?"

Hilary was quiet. Then she said, "Veronica, I want to take pottery lessons. I'm excited about it."

"That's exactly what I mean," Veronica snapped. "That's the most selfish thing I've ever heard of. I mean, I would understand if someone were *forcing* you to take all those lessons. But you have fun. You never think the least little bit about me."

Veronica wanted to take lessons, too, but when

she asked her mother about karate, her mother said, "It's not exactly lady-like."

And about ballet — "You're not the type, Veronica. You're not delicate enough. Besides, Barbara can't spend her time keeping track of you. She has a lot of studying to do for her law degree."

Veronica had begged her mother for horseback riding lessons. Kimberly Watson took riding lessons every day after school — but, "You might get hurt, Veronica. That's all I need — doctor bills."

Hilary sighed. "Well, even though I don't have any time after school, we'll still have weekends."

"Weekends. Ha!" Veronica said. "Anyway, it just so happens I am busy this Saturday and Sunday."

"What are you doing?" Hilary asked.

"I can't talk about it," Veronica said, and she opened her mathematics book.

"Is everything all right?" Hilary asked.

Veronica nodded and decided that Hilary did not deserve to know the secret.

A new girl was moving into the apartment next door to Veronica on Saturday. Veronica had never met her, but Veronica's mother had met her parents. "A stunning couple, but a bit reserved. Their name is Webb — Blanche and Arthur Webb. I asked them if they were any relation to the Philadelphia Webbs, but it seems they are not . . ."

Crystal Webb was the same age as Veronica, and Veronica thought she had a beautiful name. Mr. and Mrs. Webb told Veronica's mother that she had been at boarding school in Switzerland, but now she would be going to Maxton Academy, Veronica's school!

Crystal was an only child, just like Veronica. *We have a lot in common,* Veronica told herself. *I'll help her adjust. I know what it feels like to be at a new school.* Veronica had entered Maxton Academy in third grade.

She thought it would be best to keep Crystal to herself all weekend, so they could become close friends before she introduced Crystal to her classmates on Monday.

She peeked over at Hilary, who was staring out the window. *And after all the time I wasted being her best friend,* Veronica thought.

Veronica had been planning to share Crystal

with Hilary, but not right away. She had pictured the three of them becoming the best of friends, but now . . . *Well, at least I'll have Crystal to play with after school.*

The bus stopped in front of Maxton Academy. Veronica could see Amy, Kimberly, and their friends standing at the top of the steps. They were all wearing identical pink ski jackets.

Kimberly was the center of attention, closely guarded by Amy. Then, there was Meg — a chubby girl with orange hair who did everything Amy told her to do; Ashley — a quiet dark-haired girl with gray eyes; and Gaby — athletic and tough. Veronica looked around for Diane, but she didn't see her.

"I'm sorry that I don't have time after school, Veronica," Hilary said, as they climbed the steps.

Veronica did not say anything.

"I guess I'll see you at lunch," Hilary said. She was in the other fifth-grade class.

Veronica turned to Hilary and said coldly, "It just so happens I have permission from my mother to eat lunch out. She wrote a note before she left on her ski trip last night. I told her I couldn't stand the lunchroom food another day."

Hilary looked up and her eyes fluttered. It was a habit that had always disturbed Veronica very much.

"Are you going out with the Seven-Up Club?" Hilary asked.

"Probably," Veronica said. "I haven't decided yet."

Amy, Kimberly, and their friends were the only ones who had permission to eat lunch outside the school grounds. They were the most popular girls in the fifth grade, and they always stuck together. There were only six of them, but they called themselves the Seven-Up Club. No one outside the club knew why.

Veronica did not even know where they ate lunch, but she figured she would just go along "as quiet as a little mouse." Veronica had made up her mind to break into Amy and Kimberly's crowd by the end of this week.

But only to help Crystal, she told herself. *I'll be in a better position to help Crystal adjust.*

She was planning to find out where they bought their pink ski jackets, so she could get one exactly the same.

But she had already decided to say "No" if they asked her to be the seventh member of the club. "I don't believe in clubs that leave people out," she would say.

Veronica sat in her classroom staring at the empty seat in the first row by the window. The Seven-Up Club always sat together, but Diane was absent today. There was no one sitting next to Kimberly.

Everyone wanted to be friends with Kimberly Watson. Kimberly was sitting in the middle of a ray of sunlight coming in through the window. Amy sat behind her, and they were whispering together. Meg and Gaby, who sat on either side of Amy, were leaning forward, listening to Kimberly. Kimberly twisted her silky blonde hair around her finger. She looked very unhappy about something.

Veronica strained her ears to hear what Kimberly was saying. She looked again at the empty seat.

"No more riding lessons?" Meg wailed. "Oh, Kimberly, I can't stand it. That's the most awful thing I ever heard."

Kimberly nodded. "Not until my marks go up."

Veronica gasped. No riding lessons. That meant Kimberly was free after school.

Veronica stared at the empty seat next to Kimberly.

Suddenly she made a decision.

Chapter 2

Eye Problems

Veronica picked up her books and moved into the empty seat.

"What do you think you're doing?" Amy asked.

"You can't sit there," Meg said. "That's Diane's seat."

Gaby said, "Move it, Veronica."

"Veronica . . ." Amy said in a warning tone.

Veronica carefully arranged her pencils and her books on Diane's desk.

"Miss Penny," Amy called out. "Tell Veronica she can't sit there."

"What seems to be the trouble?" Miss Penny asked.

"That's Diane's seat," Amy said. Then in an undertone she said, "Diane will be furious if she ever finds out that Veronica the Show-off sat there."

There were giggles.

"Veronica who?" Miss Penny asked. She was a mousey young woman with straight brown hair, a large chin, and big glasses with pink frames. The corners of her mouth were always turned down.

"Veronica . . . um . . . Schmidt," Amy said.

"Veronica, I think it would be best if we kept our own seats," the teacher said.

Meg called out, "Miss Penny, I can't see over Veronica's head. She's too tall."

"Her head's too fat," Amy muttered. There were more giggles.

"I don't see why she can't sit there," Veronica heard Kimberly whisper.

Veronica sat down and stared at Kimberly. She had always suspected Kimberly liked her — that Kimberly wanted to be her friend — but Amy had some mysterious power over her.

Veronica decided to hold her ground.

"Veronica, please take your own seat. We are

using up the time for our math test."

"Miss Penny, I have to sit here. It's an emergency."

Veronica had made a New Year's Resolution not to tell any more lies. But lies seemed to pop out of her mouth before she could stop them. Finally she had allowed herself one lie a week. Unfortunately, she had already told this week's lie to Barbara. She had told her she had to watch her favorite soap opera, *Twilight of Darkness*, every afternoon for an English report.

Veronica was afraid that, with only one lie a week, she had gotten out of practice. She took a deep breath. "Yesterday morning I had to be rushed to the eye doctor. . . ."

"Yesterday was Sunday," Amy called out.

"Please, Amy. Let Veronica continue."

"It was the most terrible thing. I woke up with these weird bubbles in front of my eyes . . . I could hardly see. . . ."

Veronica squinted to prove she was having difficulty even seeing Miss Penny.

"The eye doctor was terribly worried and he said I might have to wear eyeglasses any minute so my eyes won't be strained. He also said I had to sit closer. . . ."

"Well, eyes are very important." Miss Penny studied Veronica. "Veronica, it would be helpful if you could bring me a note from the eye doctor, and we'll see what we can do. In the meantime you may stay in Diane's seat."

Amy groaned, Meg groaned, and Gaby groaned. Veronica glanced at Ashley and wondered why Ashley didn't groan. *Maybe Ashley likes me, too,* she thought.

Veronica turned and whispered to Kimberly. "Guess what, I don't have lessons after school either. I'm free this afternoon."

"Shut up, Veronica," Amy said.

But Veronica went on, "I have permission to eat out, too."

Kimberly just smiled dreamily at Veronica. She seemed to be thinking about something else.

Veronica settled herself into the seat. She felt warm and comfortable in the circle of sunlight.

Miss Penny handed out the math test. It was on decimals.

For the next ten minutes, Veronica worked on

the problems. They were not difficult. She had studied enough.

She had an odd feeling that she was being watched. She glanced over at Kimberly. To her surprise, Kimberly was staring at her paper.

Veronica looked around for Miss Penny. Miss Penny was standing at the door talking to Wingate Craven, the headmaster of Maxton Academy. Her face was all flushed, and Veronica thought she didn't look so mousey right at that moment.

Kimberly was still looking at Veronica's paper.

She's just daydreaming, Veronica told herself. But she didn't think she should make it easy for Kimberly to see her answers. What if Kimberly copied one of them by mistake?

Veronica tried to cover her paper with her arm in a casual sort of way. But she found it difficult to cover her paper and write with the same arm.

Besides, it was bad manners to accuse Kimberly of trying to see her paper. Veronica did not want to be rude. She didn't think she was being fair to jump to conclusions. Kimberly probably didn't even realize that her eyes were resting right on Veronica's paper.

"Write bigger," Kimberly whispered.

A shadow crossed over Veronica's desk.

Veronica shivered and looked up. She had expected to see Miss Penny standing above her, but it was only a cloud blocking the sunlight coming in through the window.

A moment later the sunlight was back, but Veronica did not feel so warm and comfortable any more. She looked thoughtfully at Kimberly.

Veronica had told many lies in her life, but she had never cheated. She didn't understand people who did. "Of course, I don't have to," she told herself. "Because I'm smart. It's easy for me."

She thought of all the pressure Kimberly must be under at home. Her father gave hundreds of thousands of dollars to Maxton Academy each year, but Kimberly had never been a good student. And then there was the new baby brother getting all the attention. . . .

Veronica suddenly felt very selfish. She moved her arm and tried to write her numbers more clearly. She would go over the test with Kimberly later, so Kimberly would understand how she *arrived* at her answers. Maybe she would even go to Kimberly's house. Veronica had only been to Kimberly's house once, to meet her new baby brother, but that time the whole class had been invited.

Veronica finished the test and looked over at Kimberly's test paper to make sure Kimberly had copied all the answers correctly.

Another shadow passed over her desk. Veronica looked up and saw Miss Penny staring down at her. The teacher had a funny expression on her face. Was Miss Penny trying to signal her? Was she trying to warn Veronica not to help Kimberly?

It seemed that Miss Penny *had* seen Kimberly copying off Veronica's paper. She interrupted the class to give a lecture on "wandering eyes."

"I expect to see your work, not someone else's work."

Veronica blushed with embarrassment for Kimberly.

"And if I catch any more wandering eyes, that person can expect a zero on this test."

Veronica looked over at Kimberly, but Kimberly was peacefully checking her answers.

"Well," Veronica thought, "Kimberly got away

with it this time. I'll have a little talk with her. About how cheating is not helping her, and stuff like that . . ."

"Need I say more?" Miss Penny asked.

Veronica looked up. To her surprise, Miss Penny was not looking at Kimberly — she was addressing her remarks to Veronica!

Chapter 3

Out to Lunch

At lunch time, Veronica went along with the Seven-Up Club. She tried to be "as quiet as a little mouse."

"Who invited Veronica?" Amy muttered, but she didn't do anything to stop her from coming.

Veronica struggled to keep her position on the sidewalk.

"Where do you usually eat?" she asked Gaby. But Gaby didn't seem to hear Veronica. Gaby pulled ahead to walk next to Ashley.

Veronica tried to walk next to Kimberly, but she was squeezed off the sidewalk by Amy and Meg. She trailed behind, looking for an opening so she could get back into the pack.

Veronica felt as if she were in a horse race. She decided to save her strength and catch up with them on the next block. She made up her mind to get a pink ski jacket as soon as possible so that she would fit in.

Veronica maneuvered for a position while they waited at the traffic light. She didn't have a chance of walking next to Kimberly, so she planted herself between Gaby and Ashley.

Ashley was studying her with cool gray eyes. Veronica tried to think of something interesting to say. She had to get Ashley's attention.

"Crystal's coming on Saturday," she told Ashley.

"Who?" Ashley seemed mildly interested.

"Crystal Webb. She's moving into the apartment next door, and she's going to Maxton. I think she'll be in our class."

"Who's Crystal Webb?" Amy turned around.

Before Veronica knew it, she was telling Amy everything she knew about Crystal Webb.

"She's been at boarding school in Switzerland, so I guess we'll have to talk French together."

They crossed the street and suddenly Veronica

found herself walking right in the center of the group. Amy was interested in everything Veronica said about Crystal. Veronica was beginning to wonder why she and Amy had been enemies for so long.

"And I was thinking of having a luncheon for Crystal . . . maybe on Sunday. You're all invited, of course."

"Diane, too?" Amy wanted to know.

"Well, yes," Veronica said.

"Who else are you inviting?" Amy asked. "Are you inviting Hilary?"

Veronica shook her head. If the six members of the Seven-Up Club were really coming to the luncheon, Hilary would not fit in.

Amy said in a confidential way, "What is wrong with Hilary anyway? What's her problem?"

"What do you mean?" Veronica asked.

Amy rolled her eyes up and fluttered them. She imitated Hilary's blink very well.

"It's just a habit," Veronica said. She felt like a traitor. "But I *was* afraid that Hilary might scare Crystal until she got used to her. Of course, I'll have to spend Saturday getting to know Crystal in private so I can help her adjust."

20

"Help her *what*?" Amy asked.

"Adjust," Veronica said.

"Veronica is going to help Crystal *adjust*," Amy told Meg.

A moment later Veronica heard Amy say to Gaby, "Veronica is going to help Crystal *adjust*. Isn't that nice?"

Gaby said, "Veronica is just the right person to help Crystal *adjust*."

The pace picked up suddenly and Veronica found herself running to keep up.

On the next block Veronica pulled up alongside Amy and Kimberly. They were laughing about something, but Veronica was too late. She had missed the joke. She took long strides to keep up. When they turned the corner, Veronica took the inside lane cutting off Amy and forcing her to walk behind.

Suddenly everyone slowed down. Once again there was no room for Veronica on the sidewalk. She found herself walking ahead and backwards, and trying to talk to Kimberly, who was still giggling.

"What's so funny?" Veronica asked, ready to laugh, too.

"I can't *stand* it!" Meg squealed and she giggled.

"What?" Veronica asked.

"I can't *stand* it," Amy said and she screeched with laughter.

Everyone seemed to have heard the joke except Veronica. Veronica had a feeling they were saying something mean about someone.

She laughed, too, and said, "I can't *stand* it!" a few times, but she did not really feel she was blending in.

It was hard to walk backwards. There were patches of ice on the sidewalk. Suddenly Veronica found herself all tangled up in a leash with a Pomeranian at one end and a tiny, delicate blonde woman wearing a Persian lamb coat at the other end.

The little dog ran around and around barking at Veronica's ankles. Veronica slipped on the ice and sat down on the Pomeranian.

It took a while for Veronica to untangle herself. After she had made sure the little dog was all right and explained to the woman that she was not in the habit of sitting on Pomeranians — in fact, she had a purebred poodle herself, and had never once sat on Lady Jane Grey — she looked up and saw tears in the woman's blue eyes.

The woman was cradling the little dog in her arms. She was talking to it in a soft voice. "My poor wittle Gabriella. Are you all wight?"

"She's fine," Veronica said, and looked around.

Amy, Kimberly, Gaby, Meg, and Ashley had disappeared.

Veronica spent a lonely lunch hour, walking around, looking in coffee shops for Kimberly and her crowd. She got back to school hungry, cold, and late. Miss Penny gave her a short lecture on "abusing her privileges."

Veronica had a feeling she had a very slim chance of being class pet.

Chapter 4

Gone With the Wind

"Veronica, what happened to you?" Kimberly asked in gym class. "We looked all over for you."

Veronica was surprised. "You did?" She stared at Kimberly. "Where did you eat?"

"At Cozy Corner."

Veronica had never heard of Cozy Corner.

"I thought you knew we'd be there," Kimberly said sweetly. "We always eat there. I'll show you tomorrow."

Then she whispered, "Veronica, I don't know what to do. I don't have a book for my book report."

"But it's due on Thursday," Veronica said.

"I know," Kimberly said. "It's just that none of

the books on the list appealed to me."

"Um, Kimberly, about the math test . . ."

Kimberly breathed, "Oh Veronica, that was so nice of you. I just don't understand decimals."

"You see," Veronica said, "the most important thing is not the answers, but how I *arrived* at my answers, so that, in the future . . ."

"Oh, I know," Kimberly said seriously. "Maybe you could show me sometime."

"Sure," Veronica said. "Why not today? I can come to your house after school. We could work on decimals."

"That is really nice of you, Veronica," Kimberly said, "but I should really work on my book report first."

"Maybe I could help you pick a book," Veronica suggested. "What do you like to read?"

"In the way of books?" Kimberly asked.

Veronica nodded.

"I guess I'm not crazy about books," Kimberly said.

Veronica loved books. She read all the time. She wanted everyone to love books.

"Well, then what *do* you like to read?" Veronica asked.

Kimberly shrugged. "Regular stuff. Magazines, love comics . . . love comics mostly."

Veronica thought about the list of books they were to choose from. Suddenly she had a brilliant idea.

"*Gone With the Wind!*" she said. "It was written by Margaret Mitchell. You would love that book. Did you see the movie?"

Kimberly shook her head. "What's it about?"

"I don't want to spoil it for you," Veronica said.

"That's okay, you won't spoil it," Kimberly insisted. "Just tell me what happens in it."

"I have a better idea," Veronica said. "We'll go to the school library right after school and check out the book. Then I can come to your house and help you with decimals and you can start the book right away — tonight."

But Kimberly told Veronica she had to go straight home after school.

Veronica said she would check out the book for her and bring it to Kimberly's house.

As soon as classes were over, Veronica went to the school library. *Gone With the Wind* wasn't on the shelf. It had been checked out.

Veronica didn't know what to do. The local

26

branch of the public library had been closed because of budget cuts. The last time Veronica had passed her local library, she had noticed that the building looked very shabby. The windows were dirty and seemed to be staring blankly into space. All her favorite books were trapped in there, including *Gone With the Wind*.

Hilary, Veronica, and another friend, Melody, had started a Save the Library Committee, but they hadn't had a meeting for a long time. Hilary had lessons all the time, Melody had a dog-walking business that kept her busy, and Veronica was beginning to give up hope.

Veronica wasn't allowed to go down to the main branch of the library by herself. She sat on the school steps and tried to think.

Then she remembered the lunch money she still had in her pocket. She used the money to buy a paperback copy of *Gone With the Wind* at the local bookstore.

She called Barbara from a public phone booth and asked the operator to reverse the charges.

"Who's calling?" Veronica heard Barbara ask the operator.

"Veronica," the operator said.

There was silence at the other end. Veronica was afraid Barbara would not accept the call.

"What do you want now?" Barbara asked. "I'm in the middle of washing my hair."

Veronica told Barbara she had to go to her friend Kimberly's house.

"I thought you had to watch that soap opera for an English report," Barbara said.

"Kimberly and I will be watching it together," Veronica said and decided her lie could count toward next week.

When Veronica arrived at Kimberly's house, it was four-thirty. She felt very hungry.

She handed Kimberly the copy of *Gone With the Wind*, and waited to be invited inside.

Kimberly stared at the book. "You don't expect me to read this. It's so fat."

"Don't worry," Veronica assured her. "Once you start it, you won't be able to put it down."

"Can you help me with tomorrow's math homework first?" Kimberly asked.

"Sure," Veronica said.

Kimberly led Veronica into the kitchen.

Veronica was a little disappointed that they had to work in the kitchen. She thought it would be cozier in Kimberly's bedroom, but Kimberly said her baby brother was napping upstairs.

Veronica stared at the shiny black refrigerator. "Did you already have a snack?" she asked. The kitchen did not look like a place for food. There were black counters and cabinets with mirror tiles on the walls.

"I'm not hungry," Kimberly said.

Veronica opened her math book and tried to make decimals interesting for Kimberly. Veronica enjoyed playing teacher, but she noticed that Kimberly's eyes were glazed over. She only perked up when Veronica got the answers to the problems. Then she copied the answers.

The phone rang. "I'll call you back," Kimberly said to someone.

Veronica felt very special.

Every day that week, Veronica helped Kimberly after school. She was allowed to go along with the Seven-Up Club for lunch. She felt quite shy and only talked when Amy asked her if she had found out anything more about Crystal Webb.

Luckily Veronica could describe all the paintings and furniture in the Webbs' apartment — the wallpaper, too. The week before she had seen the door open and had gone inside. She had wandered around the apartment and frightened the interior decorator very badly. The interior decorator was not interested in Veronica's many suggestions for Crystal's room — even when Veronica showed up the next day with wallpaper samples.

He had closed the door in Veronica's face and muttered something about "having to check with building security."

"I'll bet Crystal's a real snob," Diane said. Diane was back at school now and she was curious about Crystal, too.

"I don't think so," Veronica said. "I think she's too shy to be a snob."

On Wednesday after they had done their math homework, Veronica asked Kimberly if she had finished reading *Gone With the Wind*.

"Not quite," Kimberly admitted. "Veronica, could you tell me just a little bit about it, just, you know, review what happens."

Veronica began: "Well, as you know, Scarlett O'Hara is in love with Ashley, but Ashley is in love with Melanie, but Melanie loves Ashley, too, but she is Scarlett's best friend. Then Scarlett falls in love with Rhett Butler. . . . Meanwhile Scarlett is going through the Civil War . . ."

"The what?" Kimberly asked.

"The Civil War. You know, when the North was fighting the South and Abraham Lincoln was President."

Veronica went on with the story of *Gone With the Wind* and then she stopped. She didn't want to spoil the ending for Kimberly.

She looked at Kimberly.

"What are you writing?" she asked.

On Friday morning Kimberly's book report was on the bulletin board. She had gotten an A+.

"Nice informal tone," Miss Penny had written.

Veronica only got a B−. Her book report was on *The Secret Garden*, by Frances Hodgson Burnett. "Try to choose something less difficult for your next report," Miss Penny had written. Veronica was very insulted.

Veronica read Kimberly's book report with a sinking feeling.

"Scarlett is in love with Ashley, but Ashley loves Melanie, etc."

They were almost Veronica's words exactly.

There were a few flourishes. . . .

"Meanwhile Scarlett is going through the Civil War, which really gets in the way of her relationships . . ."

At the end Kimberly had written, "I'd rather keep the ending a secret. I wouldn't want to spoil the book for other people."

"Nice touch," Miss Penny had written.

That afternoon Veronica made Kimberly swear to read all of *Gone With the Wind.*

"Oh, I will. But I want to read it for pleasure, now that the book report is over." Kimberly seemed very happy.

"I'll have to test you on it," Veronica said.

"Oh fine," Kimberly said. "You can test me on it on Sunday after the luncheon."

"The luncheon?" Veronica asked.

"The luncheon you are having for Crystal."

"You mean the luncheon is on? Is everyone coming?" Her mother was still away and Veronica hadn't even asked Barbara if she could have a luncheon.

"Of course," Kimberly said. "We all want to meet Crystal. What time do you want us to come?"

"One o'clock," Veronica said, trying to imagine

the most popular girls in her class coming to *her* apartment. "Uh, Kimberly, how come the Seven-Up Club is called the Seven-Up Club?"

"Huh?" Kimberly asked.

"There are only six of you," Veronica said.

"That's right. We haven't chosen the seventh member," Kimberly said. "Every Saturday afternoon we have a meeting and discuss a different person who we might ask to be in the club, *if* they improved, of course. We have to discuss their bad qualities and their good qualities — mostly their bad qualities," Kimberly admitted.

"Oh," Veronica said, and wondered if her name had come up yet.

Kimberly looked at Veronica with horror. "Oh, Veronica, I'm not supposed to tell anyone what I just told you. It's one of the HIGH SECRETS of the club."

"I won't tell anyone," Veronica promised.

"You're a really good friend," Kimberly said, looking up at the clock.

They worked on their homework for Monday. The phone rang and, once again, Kimberly told the person at the other end that she'd call back.

The homework for Monday was hard. Kimberly

watched Veronica struggle with the problems. Then she sharpened her pencil and neatly copied what Veronica had figured out.

It was time to leave. Kimberly did not walk Veronica to the door. While Veronica was putting on her jacket, she decided she would ask Kimberly what she should serve at the luncheon for Crystal.

When she got to the kitchen door, she heard Kimberly talking on the phone. She stood there and waited for Kimberly to get off the phone.

Kimberly was talking to Gaby.

"What's-her-face finally left," Kimberly said. "I thought I'd never get rid of her. Are you ready? The answer to the first problem is . . ."

Kimberly was giving Gaby the answers to the math homework — Veronica's answers.

Veronica left in a hurry.

Veronica felt she had been betrayed. She sat on the bus furious with herself for all the time she had wasted that week trying to help Kimberly. She was sorry she had invited Kimberly and Gaby to the luncheon.

Now she had less than a day to get ready to welcome her true friend — *someone who will like me for my own self*, Veronica thought.

From the window of the bus she could see the first star of the evening twinkling faintly in the sky.

"Crystal Webb . . ." she whispered. "Crystal is coming. . . ."

Chapter 5

The Welcome Committee

All Friday evening Chris heard shuffling and scraping sounds in the hallway. He knew that Veronica was up to something.

Christopher Miles had lived across the hall from Veronica for years. Veronica had been in his class in first and second grades when she had gone to public school.

Chris was curious, but he was afraid even to look through the peephole. He didn't want to be roped into another one of Veronica's projects.

For the past few weeks Veronica had told all her plans for their new neighbor to Chris. She had even asked him to be on her Welcome Committee. "Just as long as you promise to fade into the background while Crystal and I get to know each other and become best friends," she had added.

"We're almost exactly alike," Veronica kept saying. "We're 'only' children . . . etc., etc., except that her parents are happily married and mine are happily divorced, which is pretty close."

"But you haven't even met her yet," Chris said. "How do you know what she's like?"

Sometimes Chris had a nightmare vision of not one, but *two* Veronicas living next door to him.

Other times, he felt sorry for Crystal.

"Veronica, are you going to jump all over her right away?" he asked.

"Of course not," Veronica snapped. "I'm going to make her feel at home."

Chris's curiosity finally got the best of him. He peeked through the peephole. The hall was decorated with balloons, crêpe paper flowers, and streamers. Veronica must have spent weeks getting everything ready for Crystal.

Veronica had rung his doorbell six times that afternoon.

At five o'clock she wanted his approval on the "Welcome Basket" for Crystal. The wicker basket had two packets of cocoa, two strawberry tarts, two mugs, two spoons, plates and napkins . . . "So she can invite me in for a little something when she arrives. They won't have unpacked and there probably won't be a thing in their apartment to eat."

At five-fifteen she came back to ask him to help her choose the menu for the luncheon on Sunday.

"I need a theme for the luncheon," Veronica said. "A theme helps break the ice, but I don't have any ideas. I was going to serve striped tomato and pea soup and bunny salad . . ."

"That sounds great." Chris held the door open so Veronica could leave.

"I'm not sure," Veronica said. "Bunny salad is really for Easter. You see, you use a hard-boiled egg for the face sitting on half a tomato for the body — carrot ears, raisins for eyes, cloves for the mouth, and a marshmallow tail."

"Serve bunny salad," Chris said.

"Doesn't it sound a little babyish?" Veronica wanted to know.

"Call it rabbit salad instead," Chris suggested, and tried to close the door on Veronica.

"Is your mother here?" Veronica asked.

"She's helping my father in the darkroom," Chris told Veronica. "He has a big job to finish over the weekend." Chris's father was a photographer.

"You see, my mother's away on a ski trip," Veronica said, "but she always wanted me to have a luncheon for my friends at Maxton. She will be delighted when she hears about it, and, of course, it won't be any work for Barbara."

"Does Barbara know you're having this party?" Chris asked.

"I haven't exactly told her about it yet," Veronica said. "She has a law exam on Monday and I don't want to disturb her." Then she said sadly, "I just wish I had a theme for the luncheon."

"Well," Chris said slowly. "Valentine's Day is two weeks away. . . ."

"No good," Veronica said. "Crystal and I will probably be putting on a Valentine's Day party together. You'll be invited to that one, Chris."

Chris sighed. The fastest way to get rid of Veronica would be to think up something in a hurry.

"I've got it!" Chris said, "Sunday is February 2nd, Groundhog's Day."

"So what?" Veronica asked.

"Don't you see?" Chris went on. "It's a very important day. On Sunday the groundhog will let us know if spring will be early."

"I know that!" Veronica said. Then she said, "How?"

"If the groundhog sees its shadow, it gets scared and goes back to sleep for the rest of the winter."

Veronica corrected him. "You mean he goes back into *hibernation.*"

Chris sighed and went on. "Yes, Veronica. But if he doesn't see his shadow, he stays out. That means spring will come in less than six weeks."

Veronica's eyes opened wide. "Groundhog's Day?" she whispered. "That's it! Oh thank you, Chris."

Veronica left in a hurry, but at six o'clock she showed up again. She handed Chris a two-page typewritten schedule of Crystal's weekend.

"It's just a draft," she said. "I can make changes. I'm a fast typist."

Chris read the schedule.

SATURDAY MORNING, February 1st

The Welcome Ceremony will take place upon the arrival of Crystal Webb in the 8th-floor hallway, to be followed by a private gathering of Veronica and Crystal at Crystal's apartment. Hot cocoa and strawberry tarts will be served.

SATURDAY AFTERNOON.

1 p.m. Visit to Veronica's apartment and introduction to pets — Lady Jane Grey (pure-bred poodle with pedigree papers), and Gulliver, her rare cat (half Persian, half Siamese, half Calico, and half Angora).

A meeting will take place on the window seat in Veronica's room. Crystal and Veronica will discuss their favorite books and how homesick Crystal is for her friends at the boarding school in Switzerland.

2 p.m. Drop in on Christopher Miles for a brief chat and introduction to his parents

and cat, Tiger (domestic short hair).

2:10 p.m. Tour of neighborhood including
the community garden, riding stable, and
other local sights. It will end on the steps of
the Harding Branch of the public library
(now closed), and Veronica will tell Crystal
about the Save the Library Committee and
make her an honorary member in a brief
ceremony.

SATURDAY EVENING.

6 p.m. Order out pizza at Crystal's,
decorate Crystal's room, play dress-up, watch
television, discuss philosophy of life, and
generally relax.

Chris took a deep breath. "You're not serious,
Veronica."

"Turn the page." Veronica was very excited.

SUNDAY MORNING, February 2nd

9 a.m. Crystal arrives at Veronica's house
for briefing on the luncheon and who will be
attending.

1 p.m. (see Invitation below)

> You are cordially invited
> to celebrate Groundhog's day
> at a luncheon at the home
> of Veronica Schmidt on
> Sunday February 2nd, at
> one o'clock. The menu will
> include striped soup and
> groundhog salad, which throughout
> history have always been
> the traditional foods served
> on this special day.

Chris stopped reading. "Groundhog salad?" he asked.

"Yes," Veronica said. "It's based on bunny salad, but you see, I'm going to dye the eggs and marshmallows brown, make little whiskers out of . . ."

Chris felt his stomach turn over, but he read on:

> As is the custom in this country,
> the luncheon will be followed by
> the annual groundhog walk through
> the park spotting groundhogs out
> looking for their shadows.

"I never heard of that custom," Chris said. "People don't really make such a big deal about Groundhog's Day."

"Well, how is Crystal going to know that?" Veronica snapped. "She has been in school in Switzerland her whole life."

Veronica was quiet for a moment. "Chris," she said. For a moment Chris thought there were tears in her eyes. "This is the most important thing that's ever happened to me, and I really want your honest opinion. Keep reading."

Chris read on about the plans for that evening's meeting when Veronica gets Crystal ready for the first day at school, helps her choose what to wear, and gives her hints on how to behave.

"Just hints," Veronica said. "I'm not going to give her advice or anything like that." She looked at Chris. "Well, what do you think?"

Sometimes Chris hated Veronica, but right at this minute, he wanted things to work out for her very badly. He felt she should hear the truth.

"Well, Crystal doesn't have a moment to herself. She might think you're trying to boss her around and control her life. I think you're overdoing it."

"Thank you for telling me the truth," Veronica

said in her most sincere voice. "I'll go make the changes. I'm getting better at taking criticism." She left.

Chris felt he had done a good job, and was happy to see Veronica a half an hour later with her revisions.

She did not push her way in. She stood in the doorway and asked politely, "Is this a good time, Chris?"

"Sure," Chris said. Veronica handed him her revised schedule.

Chris went into the living room and sat down to study it carefully. It seemed to be exactly the same.

"You see? You see?" Veronica asked excitedly. "I can't tell you how much you helped, Chris. I owe it all to you."

Chris couldn't understand it. "Don't you see how much I left out?" Veronica asked.

Veronica pointed out that playing dress-up was no longer on the schedule. "Crystal might think it's a little babyish," Veronica said. She had also added a ten-minute rest period during which they would return to their own apartments on Saturday afternoon.

"Will you help me put up the Welcome sign in the hallway tomorrow morning?" Veronica asked. "I'll have to borrow your ladder."

"I'm not sure," Chris said. "My friend Danny is coming over."

"Who's Danny?" Veronica wanted to know. "Aren't you friends with Peter anymore?"

Chris and Peter were not talking to each other. Chris had become interested in baseball and the history of baseball, and Peter had called him a moron.

But it was none of Veronica's business.

"Then you and Danny can help me hang the sign," Veronica announced.

Chris gave up. He didn't know what to say. All he could think about was the nightmare he had been having for the last few weeks.

What if there were two Veronicas!

Chapter 6

Groundhog Salad

At seven o'clock Saturday morning Veronica was in the kitchen preparing groundhog salad. The luncheon wasn't until Sunday, but Veronica wanted everything ready ahead of time. Everything had to be under control before the arrival of Crystal this morning.

She put the eggs on to boil and heated a saucepan full of coffee to dye them brown. She cleared everything out of the refrigerator and set it on the kitchen counter.

Barbara had left her notes and papers spread all over the kitchen table. She had been up late studying for her law exam.

Veronica needed the space, so she carefully put the notebooks and papers in a pile and looked around for some place to put them while she laid out plates for the individual salads.

She decided to put Barbara's papers on the bottom shelf of the refrigerator for the time being. Then she laid out her mother's best plates on the kitchen table. Six plates for the six members of the Seven-Up Club, another one for Crystal, and one for Veronica. Eight in all.

She set the kitchen timer and looked at her list of things to do:

Set dining room table for party.
Wash Lady Jane Grey.
Brush Gulliver.
Get dressed and wash own hair.
Put out Welcome Basket and decorate hall.
Hang Welcome sign.

Veronica knew she would need Chris's help for the sign. Well, she would need Chris's ladder, anyway.

The night before, in a fit of generosity, Veronica had made a new Welcome sign out of a big sheet:

VERONICA AND CHRIS WELCOME YOU

Underneath was the same message in French:

VERONICA ET CHRIS VOUS
SOUHAITE LA BIENVENUE

to make Crystal feel more comfortable.

Veronica studied her recipe for groundhog salad. Brown hard-boiled eggs for the bodies, marshmallows dyed brown in soy sauce for the heads, eyes made of cloves, tiny white jelly beans for the teeth, raisin ears, and cut-up licorice string for the whiskers. The tails were a problem but Veronica had finally decided to use beef jerky.

Veronica went to set the dining room table for the party. She was excited. This was her first party since she had come to Maxton Academy in the third grade. *And it's about time,* she told herself.

She had made place cards with each guest's name and she put a place card in front of each setting. She would sit next to Crystal, of course, and Kimberly would sit on the other side of Crystal. No. She didn't want Crystal and Kimberly to become too friendly right away, so she changed the place cards and put Ashley next to Crystal instead. Veronica made sure Amy and Kimberly did not sit next to each other. In fact, she put Amy way at the end of the table next to Meg.

The timer for the eggs went off and Veronica went to the kitchen.

By eight o'clock Veronica had the eggs in a bowl of coffee and the marshmallows in soy sauce. She placed the two bowls on the top shelf of the refrigerator. She arranged parsley and lettuce on each plate and hoped it would not wilt by Sunday.

She heard a noise and looked around. Barbara was standing behind her in her white kimono. Her streaked blonde hair was in big rollers and she had a mask of green clay on her face. Every Saturday morning Barbara gave herself a beauty treatment.

"Where are my notes?" she mumbled. Her face was stiff from the green clay mask and she had trouble moving her mouth.

"I put them in a safe place," Veronica said. "I'll get them in a minute."

"How dare you touch my notes," Barbara muttered. She stared at the plates. "What are you doing?" she asked.

"I'm making salad for the luncheon tomorrow," Veronica told her.

"What luncheon?" Barbara asked. "Who said you could have a luncheon?"

"Didn't my mother tell you about it?" Veronica asked, trying to look very surprised. "She gave me permission before she left."

"No one said a word to me about any luncheon. I'm not getting paid for this. Where are my notes?" Barbara was beginning to sound a little hysterical. "Get them right this minute. Do you know how important this exam is to me?"

Veronica noticed that cracks were beginning to spread around Barbara's mouth in the dried green clay.

"Where did you hide my notes, you little brat?"

Veronica sighed. "Look in the refrigerator," she said.

Barbara opened the refrigerator door and shrieked. She shrieked again.

"What's in those bowls? What's that revolting mess?"

"Be careful," Veronica said. "Don't touch it. It's groundhog heads and groundhog bodies."

Barbara stood in front of the refrigerator, with her mouth open, but no sounds were coming out. The cracks in her green clay mask were spreading up her cheeks and around her forehead.

"You're ruining your facial," Veronica said in her most considerate voice. She collected Barbara's notes and notebooks from the bottom shelf and handed them to Barbara.

Barbara turned and walked stiffly out of the kitchen. "I don't need this. I don't need this," she said over and over. A moment later Veronica heard her slam the door to her room.

Veronica spent the next two hours peacefully washing her white poodle and brushing her cat, Gulliver. She went through her mother's clothes closet and picked out a blue-and-gold silk hostess robe to wear to greet Crystal.

Veronica was big for her age. Her mother was slender, but the robe was loosely cut. It dragged along the floor a little. She brushed her thick, shiny, dark hair and tucked it behind her ears.

Veronica checked on the Welcome Basket next to the doormat at the Webbs' apartment. She hoped the strawberry tarts would not be stale by the time Crystal got there.

She dragged a small glass table into the hallway and put a clipboard with Crystal's schedule for the weekend and the invitation to the party on it. She brought the big sheet with the Welcome message into the hallway along with a hammer and some nails. Then she rang Chris's doorbell. She was ready to hang the Welcome sign.

Chapter 7

Crystal!

Chris's mother answered the door. She was wearing a heavy blue smock.

"Oh Veronica, I'm working in the darkroom right now. Chris's father has a big photography job due on Monday." She looked very tired. Then she caught sight of the decorations in the hallway. She gasped. "What's all this?"

"Crystal Webb is arriving today," Veronica told her. "Our new neighbor. There's going to be a Welcome Ceremony."

Chris's mother smiled. "You certainly went to a lot of trouble. I wish I could help."

"I just need Chris," Veronica told her, ". . . and the ladder."

"Chris went to meet his friend Danny to look at some new baseball cards at Sherman's Toy Store."

"When will they be back?" Veronica asked.

"I'm not sure," Chris's mother said.

Veronica panicked. She had to get the Welcome sign up. "May I borrow the ladder now?" she asked Chris's mother.

"Well, yes, but you're not going to climb in that robe, are you?"

"Of course not," Veronica said. "Barbara is going to help me hang the sign."

Chris's mother brought the ladder into the hallway.

"I'll bring it back as soon as I've finished," Veronica promised. Then she waited for Chris's mother to close the door.

She opened the ladder, hitched up the silk robe, and climbed up, dragging the Welcome sign behind her. She nailed one end of the sign above Crystal's door. Then she climbed down and moved the ladder in front of the elevator.

She picked up the other end of the sheet and

climbed the ladder again. Just as she was nailing the other end of the sign into the wall, the elevator door opened.

Chris and his friend Danny walked out under the ladder.

"Veronica, what are you doing?" Chris asked, staring up at Veronica.

"Is that Veronica?" Danny whispered. "Is that the Veronica you told me about?"

"Look, Chris," Veronica called down, "Crystal may be arriving any minute. You won't have time to learn all the words to the Welcome song by heart, but you certainly can learn the chorus. There's a sheet of paper over there on the glass table. . . ."

But Chris was reading the Welcome sign. "What do you mean, VERONICA AND CHRIS WELCOME YOU?" he asked in a horrified voice.

"It's nice, isn't it?" Veronica said proudly, "and, in case you don't know, underneath is the same thing in French."

"Take it down," Chris said abruptly.

"Don't be silly," Veronica said. "You ought to be happy I'm giving you credit, too. You know, you didn't help all that much on the Welcome Committee."

"Take that sign down right this minute." Chris sounded frightened. "I didn't give you permission to use my name."

Danny was watching the elevator light.

"The elevator just went down," he said.

"That's probably Crystal!" Veronica tried to climb down, but her legs had become twisted in the blue-and-gold silk gown. "Um . . . Chris, could you help me? I'm all tangled up."

They could hear voices in the elevator.

Veronica gasped. "Chris, please help me down!"

"Let's get out of here," Chris said to Danny and the two boys made a dash for the fire exit at the end of the hall.

Veronica was stranded on top of the ladder.

A minute later the elevator door opened and a small Pomeranian stepped out, followed by the tiny blonde lady in the Persian lamb coat. It was the same Pomeranian Veronica had sat on the day she went out with the Seven-Up Club.

The little dog began running around the base

of the ladder, yapping up at Veronica.

"Gabriella! You'll hurt yourself." The delicate woman picked up Gabriella. "Arthur, someone left a ladder right in the middle of our hallway." She stared blankly up at Veronica. "Arthur, someone's on top of the ladder." She caught her breath. "And, Arthur, she's wearing a Mary Stuart original!"

A tall, elegantly dressed man stepped out of the elevator, carrying two heavy suitcases. As he passed under the ladder, he looked up at Veronica and winked.

Blanche Webb had lost interest in the ladder and the designer robe. "Arthur, hurry up and open the door for me and poor Gabriella."

"Coming, Blanche."

"Gabriella and I have to lie down immediately. We're completely exhausted."

Veronica watched Arthur help Blanche Webb into their new apartment.

"This is not the color paint I had in mind for the foyer," she heard Blanche Webb say. "Arthur, did you hear me?"

But Arthur Webb was standing outside the doorway, looking up at Veronica.

"Are you all right up there?" he asked.

Veronica shook her head. She couldn't speak. Arthur Webb was the most handsome man she had ever seen. He had a square jaw and a far-away look in his blue eyes. *Like an airline pilot,* Veronica thought.

"Can I help you down?" he asked, and gallantly he helped Veronica down the ladder. He folded the ladder for her and leaned it up against the wall.

"Crystal's on her way up. Wait until she sees this." He gave Veronica a boyish grin, winked again, and went into their apartment.

Crystal's father seemed extremely nice, but Veronica was afraid Blanche Webb wouldn't let Veronica anywhere near Crystal once she realized who Veronica was. She had a feeling Crystal was going to be tiny and delicate like her mother.

Little people always made Veronica feel like an enormous lump.

Once again the elevator was on its way up!

Suddenly Veronica wanted to run away and hide behind the fire exit with Chris and Danny.

She stood frozen to the spot and stared at the floor. The elevator door opened.

Two black rollerskates rolled out carrying a

large girl in a gray and pink plaid dress. The girl was wearing a pink ski jacket — the same ski jacket the members of the Seven-Up Club wore.

"Well, I'm here," Crystal Webb said. "You must be Veronica."

The two girls stared at each other. *We could be twins,* Veronica thought.

Crystal was big for her age like Veronica. She had the beginning of a bustline. Veronica tried not to stare at her chest. Crystal had the same coloring as Veronica. She wore her dark hair the same way — short and tucked behind her ears. Her cheeks were rosy and she had big brown eyes with very long lashes that threw shadows on her cheeks.

Veronica could not think of a single thing to say. She forgot her Welcome speech.

Crystal looked around the hallway and nodded. "I must say I am impressed," Crystal said. "What's that say?" and she pointed to the French part of the sign.

Veronica was surprised Crystal did not understand French. Maybe she had gone to school in the German part of Switzerland.

Crystal skated over to the table and picked up the clipboard.

"Is this for me?" she asked.

Veronica nodded.

Crystal read the first page and then flipped it over. She read the next page.

Veronica held her breath.

Finally Crystal looked up. "This is brilliant," she told Veronica. "You only left out one thing."

"What's that?" Veronica whispered.

"Playing dress-up," Crystal said. "I like to play dress-up."

"So do I," Veronica said.

Chapter 8

Crystal's Reply

"The dog of my dreams," Crystal said, "is a Kerry Blue Terrier. Do you know what a Kerry Blue looks like?"

"Of course," Veronica said. "I've studied dogs for years."

Veronica and Crystal had finished their strawberry tarts and hot cocoa. Crystal had asked if they could share the Welcome Basket at Veronica's apartment instead of at her own. Her parents wanted to get settled. "And I don't feel like unpacking yet," she said.

Veronica was delighted.

They were sitting in Veronica's room discussing

their plans for the future. Who they would marry, names for their children, careers . . .

"I'm going to be a librarian," Veronica said. "Definitely."

Crystal gasped. "That's exactly what I am going to be."

"We'll go to library school together. We'll open a library — a magnificent library," Veronica said dreamily, "with courtyards and rose gardens and big trees to read under. . . ."

Veronica looked at Crystal, who was sitting on Veronica's bed. Lady Jane Grey was sitting at Crystal's feet and Gulliver was curled up next to Crystal letting himself be stroked. Crystal sighed. "Maybe I'll have two Kerry Blue Terriers and a poodle just like Lady Jane Grey."

"Don't you like Pomeranians?" Veronica asked. "Gabriella seems like a nice dog."

"Ugh," Crystal said. "Gabriella is the most spoiled dog in the world. Mom lets her eat at the table and sleep in her bed. Every spring Gabriella has a collection of spring hats designed especially for her."

Veronica felt nervous. "Um . . . by any chance, did your mother say anything about me?"

Crystal looked puzzled. "What do you mean?"

"Did she say anything about . . . um . . . having met me before?" Veronica was now very worried that Blanche Webb might put a stop to their friendship if she thought Veronica was the sort of child who went around squashing Pomeranians. She decided to tell Crystal the whole story.

Crystal listened and then she said abruptly, "Don't worry. I won't say anything. My mom is awful with people. She never remembers names and faces, only the clothes they are wearing. She loves clothes."

Veronica felt relieved. "My mother likes clothes, too. They have a lot in common."

Crystal reached down and petted Veronica's white poodle. "Gabriella is my mother's dog. She's not really my dog. I guess I don't really care very much about her."

"Well," Veronica said, "my pets are your pets."

"Thank you, Veronica," Crystal said.

Crystal went to change her clothes and came back with an envelope for Veronica. It was a formal note. Veronica opened it.

Crystal Webb
accepts with pleasure
the kind invitation of
Veronica Schmidt
to attend
the Groundhog Day luncheon
on Sunday, February 2nd.
She will arrive promptly
at one o'clock.

P.S. "Groundhog's Day" is officially
incorrect. It's "Groundhog
Day." But, since the day
belongs to the groundhogs...

The reply went on and on.

At two o'clock Veronica took Crystal on a tour of Chris's apartment. Chris and his friend Danny had already met Crystal in the hall. Veronica had pulled the two boys out from behind the fire door where they had been hiding during the Welcome Ceremony and had introduced them both to Crystal. Veronica had been slightly embarrassed at the way the two boys had stared at Crystal's chest.

To her surprise, Chris opened the door with his hair neatly combed. He was wearing a jacket and a tie. He and his friend Danny (also in a jacket and tie) followed Veronica around as she showed Crystal his apartment.

"I would show you the darkroom," Veronica told Crystal, "which is extremely interesting, but right now Chris's mother and father are busy printing photographs in it."

Veronica gave Crystal quite an extensive tour. She nearly died when she heard Chris whisper to Danny, "Did you see her bumps?"

"Shh," Danny said.

Luckily Crystal didn't seem to hear what they said.

Veronica opened the closet in Chris's room and a whole bunch of babyish toys fell out.

"I was just getting ready to give those away," Chris murmured.

Then Veronica dragged Chris's cat Tiger out from under his bed and introduced him to Crystal.

When Crystal saw the collection of baseball cards on Chris's desk, she said, "You have so many Red Sox. I've wanted Luis Tiant for years."

"You collect baseball cards?" Chris asked in amazement. Crystal nodded and said she would bring them right over.

While Crystal went to get her cards, Veronica gave Chris and Danny a brief lecture on "looking a person in the face" — a lecture they did not seem to understand.

Veronica tried to be patient while Crystal, Danny, and Chris talked about baseball.

After they had returned to Veronica's room, Veronica said, "I didn't know baseball was so popular in Switzerland."

For a moment Crystal looked startled.

Veronica said, "I guess you miss your friends at the boarding school."

Crystal stared right at Veronica and then looked away. Suddenly Veronica had a feeling Crystal was hiding something. "You don't have to talk about it," Veronica said. She was curious. Had something terrible happened to Crystal at the boarding school in Switzerland?

"I don't really have any friends," Crystal mumbled.

"That's the way I always feel!" Veronica said. "Even though, of course, it isn't true. There are certain people who resent my popularity, as you will see on Monday. It only *seems* as if I don't have any friends."

The telephone rang.

Veronica picked it up.

"Is she there?" It was Kimberly. "Did Crystal Webb get there yet?"

"Yes," Veronica said, "but we're in the middle of a discussion right now."

Veronica couldn't believe she was talking this way to Kimberly Watson, but she wanted to impress Crystal. "I'll call you back, Kimberly, all right?"

"No," Kimberly said. There was a pause. "Well?"

"Well what?" Veronica felt embarrassed.

"What's she like?" Kimberly asked.

"Nice," Veronica said. She could hear other voices in the background.

"Are you still having that luncheon tomorrow?" Kimberly wanted to know.

"Yes," Veronica said.

"Look, the Seven-Up Club is meeting right now," Kimberly told Veronica. "And Amy says she doesn't want to come to the luncheon for Crystal if it's at your house. She says we should all meet for ice cream at a coffee shop or something."

"The luncheon is here," Veronica said. "That's where it is. At my apartment."

She felt nervous.

"Oh," Kimberly said. "Just a minute."

Veronica heard a discussion going on in the background. She could hear Amy's voice, but she couldn't make out what Amy was saying.

"What's going on?" Crystal asked.

"The luncheon," Veronica said. "We've got to have that luncheon! Groundhog's Day is a big holiday in this country — almost like Thanksgiving."

To Veronica's surprise, Crystal was amused. "Oh, come on, Veronica," she said.

Kimberly was back on the phone. "Look, Veronica, Amy's not coming and the rest of us will only come on one condition . . ."

The other five members of the Seven-Up Club would have to meet Crystal first outside the building to see if they liked her.

Kimberly went on to describe how they would sit at the luncheon . . . IF they decided to come.

When Kimberly had finished, Veronica was quiet. She knew Crystal was watching her, but she felt so humiliated she couldn't look up.

"Veronica," she heard Crystal whisper. "I don't really want to meet anyone yet. I'm not ready. Can't we just spend a quiet Groundhog Day together?"

Veronica smiled, took a deep breath, and said to Kimberly, "The luncheon is called off."

Kimberly was very surprised. "But . . ."

"Excuse me, Kimberly," Veronica said. "I have to get back to my guest."

When Veronica got off the phone, Crystal gave her a big hug.

Chapter 9

The Climbing Trees

It was just as well that the luncheon was called off. As it turned out, Barbara had thrown out all the preparations for the groundhog salads.

But Crystal wanted to hear about the salads. She laughed when Veronica told her the story. Veronica was afraid Crystal was going to choke on her laughter.

"Tell me again," Crystal screamed. "Tell me about their little tails."

Suddenly Veronica wanted to tell Crystal the truth about everything. Before she knew it, she had pulled out all her school yearbooks and was telling about everyone in her class — how Amy had always hated her, Hilary's lessons, and how she had always wanted to be friends with Kimberly.

"But I don't see why everyone wants to be friends with Kimberly," Crystal said. She seemed very interested in all the intrigue.

"Because, for one thing, she's beautiful."

"You call that beautiful?" Crystal stared at the picture. "She looks flaky."

"Well, she is a little flaky," Veronica admitted.

"You're ten times prettier," Crystal said.

Veronica took Crystal on a short tour of the neighborhood. She showed her the riding stables and the community garden.

Crystal was horrified that the Harding Branch of the public library was closed down.

"This is shocking!" she kept saying.

Veronica told her about the fund-raising events and all the letters the Save the Library Committee had written.

"It's just me, Hilary, and Melody Hicks," she told Crystal. "But so far nothing has worked."

*   *   *

At five o'clock on the steps of the rundown building, Crystal Webb made a solemn pledge to help open the library.

Later, Veronica and Crystal got a pizza and brought it back to Veronica's apartment. Crystal still did not feel like unpacking so they played dress-up. Veronica dressed up as Snow White and sang, "Some Day My Prince Will Come." Crystal dressed up as the wicked stepmother.

Early Sunday morning Crystal arrived with two pairs of opera glasses — "to spot groundhogs" — the Sunday paper, and three cinnamon pastries — one for Barbara.

Barbara was touched. She even sat down with them in the kitchen, ate her pastry, and read the engagement section while Veronica and Crystal read the funnies.

It was sunny and cold in the park. They spent hours tracking "the mysterious groundhog," as Crystal called it. They developed a special "groundhog call" — a low growl, three hoots, and five screeches followed by a yodel — but with little success.

They stopped at the duck pond and looked for ducks.

"Let's go on the climbing trees," Crystal said.

"How did you know there were climbing trees?" Veronica asked in surprise. "You can't even see them from here."

Crystal shrugged. "There are usually climbing trees near a duck pond."

Veronica looked at Crystal. Suddenly Veronica had a strange feeling that Crystal knew her way around — that she was familiar with the park.

"Have you been here before?" she asked.

Crystal shook her head.

"Maybe in a previous life?" Veronica suggested.

Crystal smiled.

Crystal and Veronica spent the next twenty minutes sitting in the climbing tree discussing previous lives, the scariest movies they had ever seen, and their dreams. . . .

Veronica felt her prayers had been answered.

She had found the perfect friend.

Chapter 10

The New Girl

"You can't wear that pink jacket," Veronica told Crystal the next morning. She was nervous about Crystal's first day at school.

Crystal didn't seem nervous at all.

"What's wrong with it?" she asked. "It's my only winter jacket."

Veronica explained that only the members of the Seven-Up Club wore that particular pink ski jacket.

"That's ridiculous," Crystal said. "I can't help it if they have the same jacket."

"Well, of course not," Veronica said, "and you have a perfect right to wear it. But . . . umm . . .

Amy will start picking on you right away. It will interfere with your First Impression."

Veronica had been full of advice about "creating a good First Impression."

"Whatever you do," she had told Crystal, "don't show off. In fact, don't talk about yourself at all. Act shy. People like shy people. If anyone talks to you, just nod your head. Or let me answer for you. Oh, and by the way, don't be too smart. People at Maxton do not like it if you're a brain."

"But I am a brain," Crystal said.

"Well, of course," Veronica said. "So am I. I'm extremely intelligent, too. The minute I was born I could lift my head and roll over. The doctor told my mother I was the most advanced newborn baby he had ever seen." Veronica took a deep breath. ". . . And that is the reason you should take my advice about that jacket."

"Because you can lift your head and roll over?" Crystal asked.

"Huh?" Veronica was not used to having a friend who teased her.

"I have an idea," Crystal said. "Why don't we just switch jackets?"

Veronica thought that was an excellent idea. "Don't worry. I can handle Amy better than you can. I'm used to her. I don't want her picking on you your first day of school."

Crystal took off the pink jacket. Veronica's green windbreaker fit her perfectly!

Veronica put on the pink ski jacket. It felt very comfortable, and, naturally, it fit. Of course she was only going to wear it to protect Crystal, but she couldn't help feeling a certain sense of belonging.

Hilary was on the bus. She was surprised to see Veronica in the pink jacket. She was even more surprised to meet Crystal Webb.

"Crystal, you'll be interested to know that Hilary is close to becoming a black belt in karate. . . ."

Veronica was about to give each girl a short biography of the other one, when Crystal turned to Hilary and said, "I'm joining your Save the Library Committee. We have to get the library to open again. I was thinking that we could have a big parade around the building. All the kids could come as the characters from their favorite books to draw attention to the situation."

Hilary smiled. She turned to Veronica. "Let's

call Melody tonight and tell her the idea."

Veronica thought it was a bit out of place for Crystal to come up with an idea to save the library when she'd only just arrived.

"Don't you think we should think about it a little first," Veronica said, "before we go rushing into anything?"

"No," Hilary said. "I think we should just do it. It's the only way we can save the library. Melody told me the library system is going to sell the building to someone who wants to turn it into a health club. We should act right away."

"Not just sit around doing nothing about it," Crystal agreed.

Veronica snapped, "We haven't just been doing nothing about it, you know. What do *you* know about all the hard work and all the struggles we have gone through ever since they closed that branch? Oh, it's easy for *you* to criticize. . . ."

"Veronica," Crystal said, "I just meant I wanted to help."

Veronica was quiet. Then she said, "It is a good idea. I think I'll come as Snow White."

Crystal grinned, "And I get to be your wicked stepmother."

She went on in a horrible rasping voice, "Mirror, Mirror on the wall, who is the fairest of them all?"

Two small children sitting across from them on the bus looked quite frightened.

"I like Crystal very much," Hilary whispered as they were getting off the bus. "She reminds me of you."

Veronica felt proud.

There was a sea of pink jackets on the school steps. Amy hung back staring angrily at Veronica, and Kimberly hovered nearby. But everyone else came over to meet Crystal.

Ashley apologized for missing the Groundhog party. "I wanted to come," she said.

Gaby came over, looked Crystal up and down, and asked her if she played field hockey.

"I'm an excellent goalie," Crystal said.

"Will you listen to that?" Amy asked Kimberly.

Crystal was not taking Veronica's advice about being modest, but everyone seemed to find her honesty amusing. Veronica was a little worried about what Crystal would say next. Crystal was laughing at Jacob's imitations of Wingate Craven, their headmaster.

Wingate Craven loomed out of nowhere and

asked Veronica to do him the honor of introducing her friend, Crystal. He shook Crystal's hand and then told her about the pleasures of hard work and intellectual achievement within their happy little family at Maxton Academy.

Veronica was proud of Crystal. For one thing, Crystal kept a straight face. In fact, she really seemed to be listening to him even though their other classmates were making faces behind his back.

"Crystal is mature," Veronica told herself. "That's why we get along."

"She's really nice," Ashley whispered to Veronica.

"Thank you," Veronica said. She felt perfectly comfortable taking the credit for Crystal Webb.

"Where did you get that jacket?" Amy demanded angrily. "Who said you could wear that? You know there is a law against impersonation."

Veronica ignored Amy.

In the classroom Miss Penny made a big fuss about Crystal. She had a desk brought in and placed it in front of Kimberly's desk. Veronica was annoyed when Miss Penny sent her back to sit in her old seat in the last row.

Everyone took out their social studies books. Veronica read the chapter about the Laplanders and began answering the questions at the end. She looked up to see how Crystal was doing.

She saw Kimberly poking Crystal in the back. Crystal turned around.

Kimberly was waving Crystal aside. Crystal looked puzzled. She turned back to her social studies book. Kimberly peeked over Crystal's shoulder. But she seemed to be finding it difficult to see anything. Kimberly gave Crystal another poke and gestured to her to move a little to one side.

Crystal suddenly caught on. "Do your own work, Kimberly," she said.

Amy sat up straight in her seat. Meg whirled around and looked at Amy.

Miss Penny looked up from her desk.

Veronica felt a shock wave go through the room.

Chapter 11

Kaleidoscope

"Veronica told her to say that," Kimberly said in a loud voice to Amy on the way to gym class. "Imagine accusing me of trying to see her answers."

"Imagine that," Amy said in a flat voice.

"What do you mean?" Kimberly sounded shocked. "Don't tell me you actually think I would ever . . ."

"Oh, come off it, Kimberly," Amy muttered. "Crystal's right. It's about time you did your own work."

Veronica looked at Crystal. Crystal did not seem

to be aware of the impact she was having her first day of school.

Crystal was an excellent volleyball player.

"Nice going," Miss Tim, the gym teacher, called. Veronica tried harder than usual that day, but her efforts went unnoticed.

Crystal had a good singing voice. Before the class was over, Miss Levy, the music teacher, assigned her a solo. Veronica had always been Miss Levy's favorite. She had gotten the lead in just about every school musical. But she decided she wouldn't mind if Crystal got the lead this spring. "People will know who she is. That's good when you're new at a school."

Crystal got along easily with people. She smiled at everyone in the hall, and they smiled back.

When people asked her, "How do you like Maxton?" she laughed and said, "Well, I'm still here."

But every once in a while she would look around for Veronica. Her face would light up as soon as she caught sight of her. Veronica felt very special.

To Veronica's surprise, Amy came over to her right before lunch.

"Are you and Crystal coming out with us to Cozy

Corner or not?" Amy wanted to know.

Veronica shook her head. "Crystal doesn't have permission to eat lunch out."

"Well, what are you going to do?"

Veronica said, "I'm going to eat in the lunchroom with Crystal."

For a moment Amy looked very unsure of herself. She went over to the other members of the Seven-Up Club. They seemed to be arguing about something.

The Seven-Up Club ate in the lunchroom that day. Ashley and Gaby sat with Veronica. Hilary and Crystal joined them with their trays. The rest of the club sat at the next table.

Veronica noticed that Amy and Kimberly did not have very much to say to one another. Everyone else was laughing at Crystal's description of Veronica's groundhog salad. Veronica felt very clever.

". . . then we found out that Barbara had thrown it out anyway," Crystal went on.

"Who's Barbara?" Ashley wanted to know.

Veronica was surprised. It was the first time that anyone at her school besides Hilary and the headmaster had shown any interest in Veronica's home life.

During recess Veronica gave Crystal a tour of the school grounds, the auditorium, and the art department. Everyone was very friendly and helpful. Veronica was surprised that so many people at Maxton seemed happy to see *her* — Veronica!

Crystal thought everything was wonderful. She kept asking questions. The drama teacher took them backstage, and the art teacher took them up to the studio where the seniors were working on special art projects. Veronica looked around at the sculptures, the paintings on easels, and up at the skylight.

That day the whole school looked different to Veronica. She had the impression of beautiful shifting patterns of colored glass—just like a kaleidoscope. But, of course, she was seeing life through new eyes — Crystal's eyes.

During study hall last period, Kimberly raised her hand and asked Miss Penny if Crystal could help her with math.

"Why don't you try, Crystal," Miss Penny said. "Use the table in the back."

A little while later Veronica heard Kimberly say, "Oh, now I see . . ."

"You do the next one by yourself," Crystal said in a no-nonsense voice.

Kimberly did.

Veronica was suddenly tired of sharing Crystal with other people.

But when Veronica and Crystal walked into the lobby of their building that afternoon, Chris and Danny were waiting for them.

Chris greeted Crystal. "We were just wondering," he said. "Do you happen to remember the result of the World Series in 1954 — between the New York Giants and the Cleveland Indians?"

"As a matter of fact," Crystal said, "I do. The New York Giants won four games in a row."

"I told you," Chris said to Danny.

Chris invited Crystal to come watch some preseason baseball on television with him and Danny. "Veronica can come, too, if she wants," Chris said.

"Sounds great," Crystal said. "Do you want to, Veronica?"

Veronica shook her head. She wanted Crystal to herself. "Maybe I should help you fix up your room," Veronica suggested.

Crystal did not seem interested in fixing up her room. "I still haven't unpacked," she said.

"Then I'll help you unpack," Veronica said. "Barbara said it would be easier if we went to your apartment today." Veronica wanted very much to be invited to Crystal's house.

Crystal went to ask her mother. Veronica heard Mrs. Webb say, "Tell Victoria this isn't a very good time."

Victoria?

She heard Crystal whisper, "It's not Victoria, mother. What's the matter with you? Her name is Veronica!"

They ended up going to Chris's house to watch pre-season baseball.

Chris and Crystal were discussing the batting order. Danny came and sat next to Veronica. "Do you understand baseball?" he asked.

"Oh, yes," Veronica said brightly. "They hit the ball and then they run."

She stared at the TV set. Chris and Crystal were deeply involved in discussing last year's pennant. Veronica suddenly had an odd feeling that she was not really there.

All at once there was a commotion outside

Chris's apartment. There was loud barking in the hallway.

"Sounds like a hundred dogs out there," Danny said.

Everyone followed Chris to the front door. He looked out the peephole.

"Dogs all over the place," he said. "All kinds of dogs."

The doorbell rang.

"Is Veronica there? I've got to talk to her right away. It's Melody! Tell her to come out."

"She's here," Chris said.

"I don't have much time," Melody called.

Veronica went into the hall.

Melody had on her jeans and her knitted hat. Her cheeks were rosy from the cold. Her eyes were a sharp blue. Chris and Danny went out into the hall to pet the dogs.

"Where is this Crystal Webb?" Melody asked. "I've got to show her something."

"I'm right here," Crystal said and came out into the hall.

Veronica began the introductions. "Crystal, this is Melody Hicks. Melody is a member of the Save the Library Committee. As you can see, she is the owner of a successful dog-walking business. She is also a close personal friend, even though she is an entire year older than me and Hilary."

"Nice to meet you, Melody," Crystal said.

Melody suddenly looked a little shy. "Hilary called me from karate and told me about the idea for a parade around the library, where everyone comes as a favorite character from a book." Melody looked at Crystal. She was a little out of breath. "So I went ahead with it."

"What do you mean, you went ahead with it?" Veronica asked.

Melody took off her knapsack and opened it. In a brown paper bag there were hundreds of flyers that said: LAST CHANCE TO SAVE HARDING LIBRARY.

Veronica read the leaflet. "This Friday afternoon?" she asked. "How can we have the parade this Friday?"

"Well, if we wait another week, it will be too late. I saw Miss Markham. She used to be the children's librarian at Harding," Melody explained to Crystal, "and she told me that the Landmarks Commission meets next Tuesday at City Hall to decide whether to designate the library as a city landmark. The people who are trying to buy the building don't want it to be a landmark. They want to remodel it as a health club."

"We've got to stop them," Crystal said.

Veronica had a strange feeling that Crystal was speaking her lines, stealing her part in a play.

Crystal read the flyer. "This is exactly right," she told Melody. "We've got to get stores to put these flyers up in their windows right now. We've got to hurry or the stores will close. I'll get my rollerskates. That will be faster."

Once again, Veronica had the strange feeling of not being there — she felt she was being replaced.

Crystal was taking over!

Melody was staring at Crystal. "You're exactly like Veronica," she said in amazement. "I only just noticed."

That made it worse. Veronica felt weird. She tried to get hold of the situation. When Crystal returned with her rollerskates, Veronica said, "We can't do this without a meeting."

"No time for a meeting," Melody said.

Veronica wanted a meeting. She had been planning to introduce a secret handshake. (The

Seven-Up Club had a secret handshake.) She had also considered suggesting requirements for new members of the Save the Library Committee. Right now anyone could join, but the only people who ever showed up were Veronica, Hilary, and Melody. She wanted it to be a little more "exclusive" to impress Crystal.

"We don't need a meeting," Crystal said. "We need action."

Veronica decided to let Crystal know she was talking to Veronica Schmidt, the Chairman of the Save the Library Committee.

"Crystal, this is all very well but it isn't enough. We've got to write up a press release right away and send it out to every radio station, newspaper, and television channel in town. . . ."

"Naturally," Crystal said. "Why don't you write up the release right now and we'll mail it out as soon as Melody and I get back."

Veronica stared at Crystal.

The elevator arrived.

Crystal and Melody got in. Chris and Danny held the door open so all the dogs could get in.

The elevator door closed behind them.

Veronica burst into tears.

Chapter 12

Eclipse

"What's the matter with Veronica?" Danny seemed very anxious.

"Why are you crying, Veronica?" Chris wanted to know.

"I don't know," Veronica sobbed. "I thought Crystal was my friend, but now she's taking over everything. I'm not even here."

"Of course you're here," Chris said nervously.

"Let me make Veronica that drink I told you about," Danny whispered to Chris.

They went back into Chris's apartment. The television was still on. Veronica couldn't stop crying. "And I don't even care about b-b-baseball," she said, and she collapsed into a chair.

"That's okay." Chris quickly turned off the TV.

"Is that why she's crying?" Danny asked. "Because she doesn't care about baseball?"

"I don't think so," Chris said.

"I'm going to make her that drink," Danny said, and he left the room.

"What happened, Veronica?" Chris asked.

Veronica took a deep breath. "Well, everyone liked Crystal so much at school. She was a big hit. I was so proud of her until all of a sudden she started taking over and running off with my friends and they all like her better than me and she's better at everything and she doesn't even try and you and Danny like her better than me because she has baseball cards and a figure and I'm not even here."

Veronica looked at Chris.

"But you are here," Chris said.

"No," Veronica said. "I've been erased."

"Wait a minute, Veronica," Chris said. "I think I know what it is, and you don't have to worry. It's just an eclipse!"

Veronica looked at Chris.

"Like an eclipse of the sun or the moon. You

see, Crystal is new so she's getting a lot of attention."

"Everyone really likes her," Veronica added.

"That's good, isn't it?" Chris asked.

"Well, yes, I want everyone to like her because she's my friend, but I want them to like me better." She thought it over. "No, maybe I don't. . . . Maybe I want them to like us both exactly the same."

Veronica felt confused.

"You and Crystal make a good team," Chris said.

"Do you really think so?" Veronica seemed pleased to hear that. She thought for a moment.

"Maybe it is like an eclipse," she finally said to Chris. "You mean that Crystal is just hiding me from view for a little while."

"That's right," Chris said. "During a solar eclipse, the moon passes in front of the sun, but the sun only seems to disappear from sight. It's still there, Veronica."

Veronica sat for a while, thinking. "Blanche Webb doesn't think I'm important enough to remember my name."

"Maybe she just doesn't remember names," Chris suggested.

"But even if I am here, no one really likes me," she said sadly.

"That's not true," Chris said crossly. "You don't even notice when people like you."

Veronica looked up. "What do you mean?"

Chris lowered his voice. "Look Veronica," he said. "I shouldn't be telling you this, but Danny likes you . . . I mean, he really likes you. He talks about you all the time. He even bought you a Valentine card!"

Veronica was speechless.

When Danny returned with the special drink for Veronica, she had trouble looking at him.

"It's ginger ale, milk, chocolate syrup, and banana," Danny said. "I invented it."

Veronica sipped the drink and stared at the floor.

Danny stood there watching her drink it.

"It's working," he said. "She stopped crying."

"It tastes nice." Veronica glanced at Danny and then quickly looked away. She knew she was blushing, but she had a nice warm feeling. . . .

Life was full of surprises.

Chapter 13

Secrets

Veronica had the press release ready that night. Crystal approved. They showed it to Barbara. She was so impressed she offered to go make copies for them. The next morning they mailed them out to every newspaper, radio station, and TV station in the city. They took an early bus to school so that they could pass out the flyers.

"What's this?" Amy asked when Veronica handed her one.

Veronica explained about the parade around the library. "You come as your favorite character from a book. It's our last chance to save the Harding Branch of the public library."

Amy did not seem to be listening.

"Um . . . Veronica," she said, "do you intend to wear that pink ski jacket from now on?" She didn't seem angry any more, just curious.

Veronica nodded. Crystal liked the green windbreaker better. They had agreed to switch.

Amy shrugged and read the flyer. A moment later Veronica heard her say to Kimberly, "Another one of Veronica's projects," and she threw the flyer into the litter basket.

Kimberly hesitated and then threw her flyer into the litter basket, too.

Crystal was furious. "Did you see that?"

Veronica explained that the Seven-Up Club had never been famous for their interest in libraries.

"Well, it's never too late to start," Crystal said. "We've got to convince them to come."

Veronica smiled at Crystal's innocence.

"We'll just be wasting our time," she said. "We've got enough to do."

"They're coming whether they want to or not," Crystal said. "Especially that Amy. I'll figure out something."

That night Crystal called every one of the members of the Seven-Up Club. "Went right down the list," she told Veronica the next morning.

"How did you get all the phone numbers?" Veronica wanted to know.

"From Wingate Craven," Crystal said. "I just went into his office and asked."

Veronica was impressed. Crystal had a lot of nerve.

"I almost convinced Kimberly to come. She said she wanted to dress up as Scarlett O'Hara in *Gone With the Wind*," Crystal sighed, "but then she said she'd have to check with Amy. When she called back, the answer was 'no.'"

"Give up," Veronica suggested gently.

Every afternoon, Veronica and Crystal went to the climbing trees in the park together to discuss life. Veronica wanted to know more about Crystal's past.

"You told me you had trouble making friends, but you seem to make friends very easily."

Crystal looked away. "I don't have trouble making friends, I have trouble . . ."

She never finished the sentence.

Keeping friends? Veronica wondered. Is that what she was going to say? But why?

Another day Veronica said, "Did something happen at that boarding school? Why don't you ever talk about it?"

"Don't feel like it," Crystal said in a voice barely above a whisper.

Veronica stayed away from the subject.

But Crystal's family life puzzled Veronica, too. Every morning she tried to see past Crystal into the apartment.

On the front hall table there was a white wicker breakfast tray with magazines in the side pockets. On the tray was a silver coffee pot and two china plates with a rose pattern. One plate had toast and butter and jam; the other plate had dog biscuits on it.

It was just the way Veronica pictured Blanche Webb and Gabriella having breakfast.

The shades were drawn in the living room. The apartment was carefully decorated, but it didn't look lived in. It was silent. Crystal always seemed in a hurry to get away from it.

Every evening that week Crystal had to be home at seven o'clock to fix herself dinner and "keep Gabriella company" while her parents went out to the theater, the ballet, or the opera.

Veronica always peeked out to see how Blanche and Arthur were dressed for each event. She thought they were the most handsome couple she had ever seen. "They would make good paper dolls," she found herself thinking.

Veronica was even more impressed when she learned that Blanche and Arthur Webb never ate dinner before eleven o'clock at night. And they always ate at the same quiet French restaurant.

"Mother is not much of a cook," Crystal said. "Dirty dishes and pots make her quite ill."

One morning Arthur Webb left for work when Veronica and Crystal were still in the hallway. He winked and said "Well, you two are hitting it off well."

"What does your father do?" Veronica asked later.

"Import-export," Crystal said.

"He's very good-looking," Veronica said. "My father is, too, but in a different way. He lives in Santa Barbara, California, and I'm sure he's going to call and tell me to bring you out there during Easter vacation."

Crystal seemed delighted with the idea. "Oh Veronica! I would love that."

"Crystal," Veronica said thoughtfully. It was Thursday afternoon. They were sitting in the climbing tree. "Does it feel funny to have brown eyes when both your parents have blue eyes?"

"What makes you say that?" Suddenly Crystal was very tense.

Veronica was sorry she had said anything, but something made her go on. "I didn't even think it could work that way. You know, I thought that if both parents had blue eyes, the child had to have blue eyes, too. . . ."

Crystal swung down from the tree and said abruptly, "I want to go see the ducks." Veronica climbed down too and ran to catch up with her.

"I'm not trying to be nosy or anything," Veronica went on, "but did it ever occur to you that you might be adopted?"

"I am not adopted," Crystal said coldly.

Veronica decided not to press the issue.

On Friday, Veronica was the only one wearing a pink ski jacket. All the members of the Seven-Up Club were wearing brand new dark green windbreakers.

"My father owns a camping store," Meg told

everyone. "He got these for us at a big discount. It's our new look."

Crystal said, "How ridiculous." She turned to Veronica. "We can switch back if you want to."

Veronica shook her head. She felt foolish in the pink ski jacket, but it would be worse to switch again. She didn't want to admit that she cared that much.

To make matters worse, Veronica was the only one at school already dressed for the parade around the library. She was wearing her complete Snow White costume, including the bow around her hair. Everyone else, including Crystal, had their costumes in paper bags.

The six members of the Seven-Up Club were not carrying paper bags.

"The only reason I'd go to that parade at the library is to laugh at Veronica," Veronica heard Amy say a few times.

Veronica noticed that Crystal spent quite a lot of time with the members of the Seven-Up Club during lunch. She even laughed at something Amy said, which annoyed Veronica.

Crystal motioned for Veronica to come over, but Veronica refused.

At the end of the last period of the day, Veronica saw Crystal standing on the steps with the Seven-Up Club. She couldn't understand why Crystal wasn't changing into her wicked stepmother costume for the parade at the library.

She waited for Crystal. She felt ridiculous in her Snow White costume and pink ski jacket. She saw Crystal put up the hood of the green windbreaker. Then she tied it under her chin so it fit very tight.

"We all have to look exactly the same," Crystal was saying, and she helped everyone adjust their hoods.

"Like this?" Amy asked.

Veronica couldn't believe her ears. She watched as the seven girls formed a chorus line with their arms around each other's waists. They danced around in a circle. Then they collapsed on the steps laughing.

Suddenly Veronica was convinced that Crystal Webb had just been invited to become a member of the Seven-Up Club!

Veronica decided right at that moment that she would never believe in anything or anybody ever again.

But Crystal had made a pact to save the library. Crystal had started this whole thing. She wasn't getting away with it. Veronica went over to Crystal and tapped her on the shoulder.

"Isn't it about time you put on your costume?" Veronica asked in a cold voice. "In case you forgot, the wicked stepmother outfit is in your shopping bag."

Crystal stopped laughing. Her face was flushed and she seemed very excited. "I'm not going to be your wicked stepmother. Boy, do I have news for you! Listen to this . . ."

Veronica couldn't listen. She ran down the steps. The bus was coming. Hilary was getting on. Hilary was dressed as Pippi Longstocking. Veronica followed her onto the bus.

There were more Pippis on the bus. In fact, the bus was full of characters from books. She passed Sherlock Holmes, who was sitting next to Robin Hood, Alice in Wonderland, Clifford the Big Red Dog, Dorothy from *The Wizard of Oz*, and Peter Pan. There was even a Little Red Lighthouse.

104

Veronica found herself squeezed between Hans Brinker and Frankenstein.

The busdriver was laughing.

Veronica felt numb.

Suddenly she heard a shout.

"Stop! Hold the bus!" It was Crystal's voice.

"Wait for us!" Amy shrieked.

The busdriver opened the bus door and Crystal, Amy, Kimberly, Gaby, Meg, Ashley, and Diane all climbed aboard. The hoods of their green windbreakers were pulled tightly over their heads.

"We're here!" Crystal called, and they all began to sing, "Heigh ho, heigh ho, it's off to work we go . . ."

"Hey, Snow White!" the busdriver called. "Your dwarfs are here."

Chapter 14

Victory

The parade at the library was a great success. It was more successful than anyone had imagined it could be.

Every television and radio station in the city was there. They interviewed Snow White and the Seven Dwarfs.

Crystal and Veronica had the most to say about the need for the library. Kimberly giggled and blushed. "I'm Dopey," she said. Everyone else, including Hilary, just stared into the television cameras.

Melody was not in costume. But her dogs were. "That's Rin Tin Tin," she explained to a television reporter. "That's Lassie. That's Toto, from *The Wizard of Oz.* . . ."

"So the dogs came as their favorite characters from books?" one radio reporter asked.

"Yes," Melody said.

In the end there were nine dwarfs. Chris and Danny showed up as Grumpy and Sneezy.

"We thought two dwarfs were better than none," Chris told Veronica. "I didn't know you already had your seven dwarfs."

"Neither did I," Veronica said.

Veronica and Crystal were watching the six o'clock news with Barbara. The anchorwoman said that the event at the library was not supposed to affect the decision of the Landmarks Commission. "They decide on the merits of the building itself," she said. "But we have just heard that the library budget will be restored. The Harding Branch of the public library will reopen!"

All three of them began to cheer.

The doorbell rang.

It was Arthur Webb. He looked very upset.

"Blanche is watching the news," he told Crystal. "She wants to talk to you right away."

"But . . . " Crystal turned pale.

"Right away," Arthur Webb said.

Crystal did not come back that evening.

Veronica heard shouting from the apartment across the hall.

"No!" Crystal screamed. "I won't. I refuse to. Not again."

Veronica stood by the back door of Crystal's apartment. It was the door to the kitchen.

She heard sobbing. Crystal was sobbing.

Veronica knocked on the door very gently.

"Crystal," she said. "Crystal, what's wrong? What happened?"

"You can't help, Veronica. I know you want to help, but you can't."

Veronica stood outside the door for hours listening to Crystal cry. Her heart ached for Crystal. She went and got a cushion and a blanket. It was cold in the hallway. She sat outside Crystal's kitchen door wrapped in the blanket.

Veronica knew that it was a private matter, but she simply could not let Crystal suffer alone.

At one point Crystal said in a voice weak from crying, "Are you still there, Veronica?"

"Yes," Veronica said.

"Thank you," Crystal said. But she didn't open the door.

When the crying finally stopped, Veronica went home. She lay awake most of the night wishing she could do something, wishing she understood.

Chapter 15

Farewell

The next morning there were suitcases and boxes in the hallway. Veronica could not believe it. The Webbs were moving out.

Crystal was dressed in the same plaid dress she had worn a week ago when she arrived. She was dragging things into the hall. Her eyes were red from crying.

"But why do you have to leave?" Veronica wanted to know. "You can't leave, Crystal." She turned to Arthur Webb. "She can't go away. She only just got here."

Arthur Webb looked very upset.

"Veronica, I'm not at liberty to talk about this. My sister feels . . ." He stopped.

Veronica knew that he had said something he had not meant to say.

"My sister feels . . ."

His sister?

Veronica said, "Are you Crystal's uncle?"

Arthur Webb didn't answer.

Crystal was staring at Veronica. Veronica knew she had guessed right.

It made sense. Blanche Webb was Crystal's mother, but Arthur wasn't her father — he was her uncle. Blanche and Arthur were brother and sister. There was a strong family resemblance.

Veronica quietly helped them move things down to the lobby. She helped load the station wagon that was parked in front of the building. She didn't know what else to do.

Blanche Webb was standing on the sidewalk in her Persian lamb coat. She was cradling Gabriella and talking to her in a baby voice. She did not turn around.

"Where are you going?" Veronica asked Crystal.

"I'll visit you. I promise I'll visit you."

"I don't know," Crystal said. Veronica knew she was telling the truth.

Arthur Webb asked if he could take a picture of Veronica and Crystal with a Polaroid camera.

"You'll have something to remember each other by."

Crystal grabbed Veronica tightly around the shoulder, and both girls looked into the camera.

"Dry your eyes and smile," Arthur Webb called.

Veronica smiled so hard it hurt.

Arthur Webb handed Veronica the photograph.

Crystal stood next to Veronica and stared down at it.

"Look at how hard I'm holding onto you," she whispered. "I never had a friend like you." She seemed unable to take her eyes off that photograph.

Suddenly she said, "Veronica, go get my roller-skates. I left them in your apartment."

"No, you didn't," Veronica said.

"Yes." Crystal said. "That's where they are. I left them under your bed."

Veronica hadn't noticed rollerskates.

But she wanted to do what Crystal asked.

She went upstairs and looked all over for Crystal's skates. They weren't there.

When she got downstairs again, Arthur Webb said, "Where's Crystal? Didn't she go up with you?"

"No," Veronica said.

"I thought that's what she said," Arthur looked upset.

Veronica said she would go upstairs to look for Crystal. "Maybe we missed each other."

"Don't worry, Gabriella," she heard Blanche Webb say, "Victoria is going to find Crystal."

Veronica whirled around. She marched back and said in her coldest voice, "In the first place, Mrs. Webb, my name is Veronica, not Victoria. In the second place, you may not think I'm a very important person, but I am. I'm important to Crystal. I happen to be your daughter's best friend. And in the third place . . ."

Veronica had not planned this speech ahead of time. She was sorry she had not stopped with "in the second place." "And in the third place," she repeated. Veronica was trying desperately to think of something.

"And in the third place, it's about time you realized that dogs are not the only people in this world."

It was the best she could do. With that, Veronica went to look for Crystal.

But Crystal wasn't upstairs. In fact, she wasn't anyplace to be found. She had disappeared.

All at once Blanche and Arthur Webb looked like two helpless children. They had once seemed like such an elegant couple. Veronica suddenly felt much wiser than either of them.

"Listen," Veronica said, "I don't know what you're both hiding from — the police or whatever it is — but I know one thing. It's wrong to take Crystal away. She's very happy here."

"I know," Blanche Webb said softly, and her eyes filled with tears. "Crystal has always needed a friend like you." She turned to her brother, "Oh, Arthur, what are we going to do? Victoria's right," and she took Veronica's hand.

Blanche Webb's hand was tiny, soft, and trusting, like the hand of a baby. All at once Veronica was sure she knew where Crystal was.

"I'll find her," Veronica promised. "I think I know where she went."

114

"I'll go with you," Arthur Webb said.

"Maybe it would be best if Victoria went alone." A look of horror crossed over Blanche Webb's fine features. "I mean, *Veronica*. Victoria was my best friend when I was a girl," she said softly. "I miss her so much."

Veronica squeezed her hand. Then she turned and ran towards the park. She headed in the direction of the climbing trees. Even from a distance she could see Crystal's plaid dress. Crystal was not surprised to see Veronica. She seemed to be expecting her.

Veronica climbed up and sat on the branch next to Crystal. She sat quietly and waited for Crystal to say something.

"I never went to school in Switzerland."

Crystal talked slowly with big pauses between sentences.

"My mother has been running away from my father for years. We've lived all over the country. I've never been in one school for more than three months."

Veronica did not talk; she just listened.

"When my mother saw me on the news last night, she got frightened again. She panicked.

She thinks my father will see me on television and find us."

"Is your father . . . um . . . violent?"

Crystal shook her head. "No, but my mother's afraid of him. Sometimes he loses his temper and yells. He wouldn't let Gabriella eat at the table with us. My mother is kind of childish about a lot of things. Maybe my father is, too. He wants to support us himself, but he doesn't make much money. He always refused to live off my mother's inheritance. She and Arthur inherited a lot of money when they were eighteen."

"Are they divorced?"

"No," Crystal said. "My mother just can't face things like that. Paperwork and lawyers and stuff like that. Veronica, I want my father to find us. I want them to settle things. I don't care if they get divorced. I just want to live in one place for a while."

"You did live here before, didn't you?" Veronica asked.

Crystal nodded. "When I was very little. It's strange how much you remember." She sighed. "We've moved so many times. I don't want to move again. I don't want to leave you."

116

"Well, then, don't," Veronica said.

"I'm tired of running away," Crystal said.

"Let's go back," Veronica said. "Let's tell them exactly what you just said — that you're tired of running away."

Crystal shrugged. "It won't do any good."

"Try," Veronica said.

Veronica and Crystal walked up the block arm in arm. Arthur Webb looked very relieved to see them. He hugged Crystal. Blanche Webb came to meet them. Her face looked tired, but happy. She handed Gabriella to Veronica and put her arms around Crystal.

"Mama," Crystal whispered. "I'm tired of running away."

"I know," Blanche Webb said.

"This time we're going to stay," Arthur said.

Crystal rested her head on her mother's tiny shoulder and closed her eyes.

Veronica and Crystal spent the afternoon unpacking. Veronica made lots of suggestions about how Crystal should decorate her room.

She went home and brought back the wallpaper

samples she had collected a few weeks before. She also brought a large stack of her mother's *House Beautiful* magazines to clip out decorating ideas. They moved the furniture around to see how it would look.

By the end of the afternoon Crystal's room was a terrible mess.

"We're never going to get it right," Veronica said. "It has to be perfect."

"All in good time," Crystal said.

Books by Nancy K. Robinson

If you enjoyed this book about Veronica and Chris, you might enjoy,

JUST PLAIN CAT
VERONICA THE SHOW-OFF
VERONICA KNOWS BEST

You might also want to read the following books about Angela, Tina, and Nathaniel . . .

MOM, YOU'RE FIRED!
OH HONESTLY, ANGELA!
ANGELA, PRIVATE CITIZEN

International crime and adventure books:

TRIPPER & SAM AND THE PHANTOM FILM CREW
TRIPPER & SAM AND DANGER ON THE SOUND TRACK
TRIPPER & SAM AND THE GHOST WHO
   WANTED TO BE A STAR

"Can-you-solve-it" series (from an idea created by Marvin Miller):

T*A*C*K TO THE RESCUE
T*A*C*K AGAINST TIME
T*A*C*K INTO DANGER
T*A*C*K SECRET SERVICE

Non-fiction books:

FIREFIGHTERS!
THE HOWLING MONKEYS
(hardcover title: JUNGLE LABORATORY)

Other fiction:

WENDY AND THE BULLIES